To Janet Jepsen who trims the tree.
To Annie Breiling who sings "Joy to the World."
To Sandra Fry who hears the song.   — E. S.

Dedicated to G. and Sonia and Ian.   — J. T-W.

SIMON & SCHUSTER BOOKS FOR YOUNG READERS
An imprint of Simon & Schuster Children's Publishing Division
1230 Avenue of the Americas
New York, New York 10020
Text copyright © 1999 by Eileen Spinelli
Illustrations copyright © 1999 by Jenny Tylden-Wright
All rights reserved including the right of reproduction in whole or in part in any form.
SIMON & SCHUSTER BOOKS FOR YOUNG READERS is a trademark of Simon & Schuster.
Book design by Lily Malcom
The text of this book is set in Gilgamesh book.
The illustrations are rendered in colored pencil with highlights added in gouache.
Printed in Hong Kong
10 9 8 7 6 5 4 3 2 1
Library of Congress Cataloging-in-Publication Data
Spinelli, Eileen.
Coming through the blizzard / by Eileen Spinelli ; illustrated by Jenny Tylden-Wright. — 1st ed.
p.   cm.
Summary: Despite a blizzard, Christmas comes to a small church in unexpected ways.
ISBN 0-689-81490-9 (hardcover)
[1. Christmas—Fiction. 2. Blizzards—Fiction.] I. Tylden-Wright, Jenny, ill. II. Title.
PZ7.S7566Co 1999
[E]—dc21
98-16795 CIP AC

Coming Through the Blizzard

A Christmas Story by Eileen Spinelli
Illustrated by Jenny Tylden-Wright

Simon & Schuster Books for Young Readers

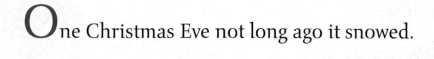

One Christmas Eve not long ago it snowed.

And snowed.

And snowed.

Snow swirled against windows,
drifted deep against doors.
Snow buried cars and park benches.
Snow blanketed the little blue church.

The minister shoveled the wide walkway.
He lit the candles.
He waited.
Who would come through the night,
through the blizzard?
Who would come to the Christmas Eve service?

The starling came
on snowy wings across a starless sky.
The starling came,
frosty and fuddled,
to huddle on a cushion in candle glow,
beneath a branch of the shining tree.
The starling came.

The custodian came
on skis, earmuffed and bundled, trundling along—
clip-clump, clip-clump.
The custodian came,
chilly and true,
to dust the pews,
to stoke the furnace,
to place the star on top of the tree.
The custodian came.

Tom Cat came,
snarly and cold,
to slouch against the bubbling radiator,
then wrestle down a red ribbon
from the hanging greens.
Tom Cat came.

The small boy came,
trailing cookie crumbs,
quilted and cozy in his mother's arms.
The small boy came
to drowse in
the sleepy scent of evergreen.
The small boy came.

Field mouse came,
on tiny icicle toes
to nose for crumbs under the pew.
Field mouse came
skating across the organ keys
away from the cat.
Field mouse came.

The organist came,
breathless and brave,
with her backpack of music
and thermos of tea.
She brushed off the keys
and tested the pedals
and blew a breath of music
through the pipes.
The organist came.

Moth came.
Silvery, silent,
blown from a pipe in the organ
on a burst of song,
a wordless Hallelujah.
Moth came.

The soloist came,
red scarf 'round his neck,
red-cheeked from the wind.
The soloist came
to add the words,
to sing "Gloria"
and "Joy to the World."
The soloist came.

A stranger came,
midnight on her shoulders,
snow on her boots.
A stranger came,
alone and shivering,
to peek past the door.
She saw the lights.
She felt the warmth.
She heard the carols.
A stranger came in.
A stranger came in.
Then . . .

Christmas came.